IN THE NIGHT KITCHEN

MAURICE SENDAK

HarperCollins Publishers

FOR SADIE AND PHILIP

DID YOU EVER HEAR OF MICKEY, HOW HE HEARD A RACKET IN THE NIGHT

AND THEY PUT THAT BATTER UP TO BAKE

A DELICIOUS MICKEY-CAKE.

SO HE SKIPPED FROM THE OVEN & INTO BREAD DOUGH
ALL READY TO RISE IN THE NIGHT KITCHEN.

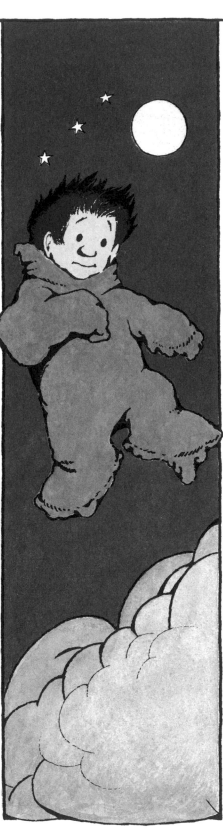

TILL IT LOOKED OKAY.

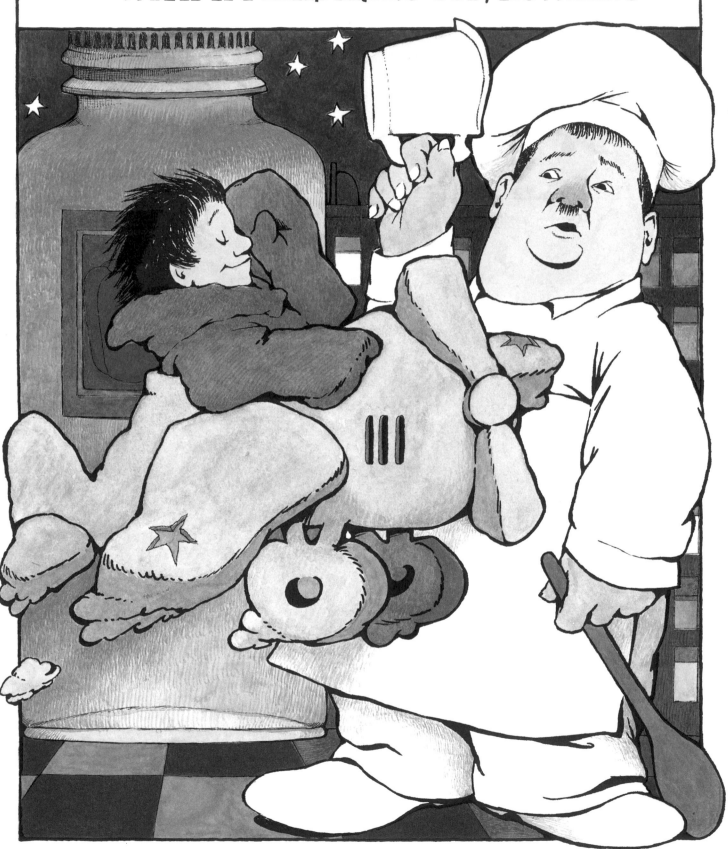

SO THE BAKERS THEY MIXED IT AND BEAT IT AND BAKED IT.